ROARING ROCKETS

Orange County Library System
146A Madison Rd.
Orange, VA 22960
(540) 672-3811 www.ocplva.org

For Danny Spiegelhalter and Virgil Tracy—T.M.

KINGFISHER
LONDON & NEW YORK

Text copyright © Tony Mitton 1997
Illustrations copyright © Ant Parker 1997
Published in the United States by Kingfisher, 175 Fifth Avenue, New York, NY 10010
Kingfisher is an imprint of Macmillan Children's Books, London.
Distributed in the U.S. and Canada by Macmillan, 175 Fifth Avenue, New York, NY 10010
Library of Congress Cataloging-in-Publication Data
Mitton, Tony.
Roaring rockets / Tony Mitton, author; Ant Parker, illustrator
p. cm.
Summary: A simple explanation of how space rockets work, where they travel, and what they do.
1. Rockets (Aeronautics)—Juvenile literature. [1. Rockets(Aeronautics) 2. Outer space—Exploration.] I. Parker, Ant, ill. II. Title.
TL782.5.M53 1997
629.47'5—dc21 97-5423 CIP AC
ISBN 978-0-7534-5305-6
Kingfisher books are available for special promotions and premiums. For details contact:
Special Markets Department, Macmillan, 175 Fifth Avenue, New York, NY 10010.
For more information, please visit www.kingfisherbooks.com
Printed in China
20 19 18 17 16

ROARING
ROCKETS

Tony Mitton and Ant Parker

KINGFISHER

NEW YORK

Rockets have power. They rise and roar.

This rocket's waiting, ready to soar.

Rockets carry astronauts with cool white suits,

oxygen helmets, and moon boots.

The countdown is finishing: 3, 2, 1 . . .

Action! Blast off! The journey's begun.

Rockets have fuel in great big tanks.

When they are empty, they drop away . . . thanks!

Up in space you're really light,

so astronauts need to buckle up tight.

Rockets go far. Through space they zoom,

reaching as far as the big, round moon.

Down comes the lander with legs out ready

and fiery boosters to hold it steady.

Out come the astronauts to plant their flag

and scoop up samples in their moon-rock bag.

Rockets explore. Through space they roam.

But when they're done, they head back home.

Rockets re-enter in a fiery flash,
to land in the sea with a sizzling splash!

The helicopter carries the brave crew away.
Three cheers for the astronauts:
Hip! Hip! Hooray!

Rocket parts

moon boots

astronauts need to wear special protective clothing when they're walking on the moon

lunar lander

this takes astronauts down from the rocket to land on the moon

oxygen helmet

we need to breathe oxygen, but there isn't any in space, so astronauts carry their own supply that flows into their helmets

fuel tanks

command module

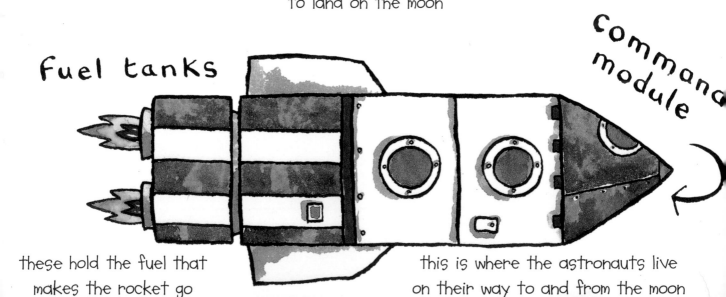

these hold the fuel that makes the rocket go

this is where the astronauts live on their way to and from the moon